Carlos & Carmen

The Nighttime Noise

by Kirsten McDonald
illustrated by Erika Meza

Calico Kid

An Imprint of Magic Wagon
abdopublishing.com

For my family and all of our nighttime noises —KKM

To my two Carlos, and specially both of my parents; who taught me to value changes, movings, carnes asadas, mischiefs, surprises and the beautiful moments you can only live with your family. Gracias: ilos quiero! —EM

abdopublishing.com

Published by Magic Wagon, a division of ABDO, PO Box 398166, Minneapolis, Minnesota 55439. Copyright © 2016 by Abdo Consulting Group, Inc. International copyrights reserved in all countries. No part of this book may be reproduced in any form without written permission from the publisher. Calico Kid™ is a trademark and logo of Magic Wagon.

Printed in the United States of America, North Mankato, Minnesota.
102015
012016

THIS BOOK CONTAINS RECYCLED MATERIALS

Written by Kirsten McDonald
Illustrated by Erika Meza
Edited by Heidi M.D. Elston
Designed by Candice Keimig

Library of Congress Cataloging-in-Publication Data

McDonald, Kirsten, author.
  The nighttime noise / by Kirsten McDonald ; illustrated by Erika Meza.
    pages cm. -- (Carlos & Carmen)
  Summary: The Garcia family has just moved into their new house, and twins Carlos and Carmen are having a hard time sleeping in their new rooms--especially when they hear a spooky noise outside.
  ISBN 978-1-62402-139-8
1. Hispanic American families--Juvenile fiction. 2. Twins--Juvenile fiction. 3. Brothers and sisters--Juvenile fiction. 4. Moving, Household--Juvenile fiction. 5. Kittens--Juvenile fiction. [1. Twins--Fiction. 2. Brothers and sisters--Fiction. 3. Bedtime--Fiction. 4. Fear of the dark--Fiction. 5. Moving, Household--Fiction. 6. Hispanic Americans--Fiction.] I. Meza, Erika, illustrator. II. Title.
  PZ7.1.M4344Ni 2016
  [E]--dc23
                    2015026228

Table of Contents

Chapter 1
New Rooms

It was the Garcia family's first night in their new red house.

The twins were each in their new separate rooms.

5

Carlos was trying to sleep in
his new green room. But his eyes
would not stay shut. He saw spooky
shadows on the walls. He saw strange
lights outside his window. But mostly,
he saw he was all alone.

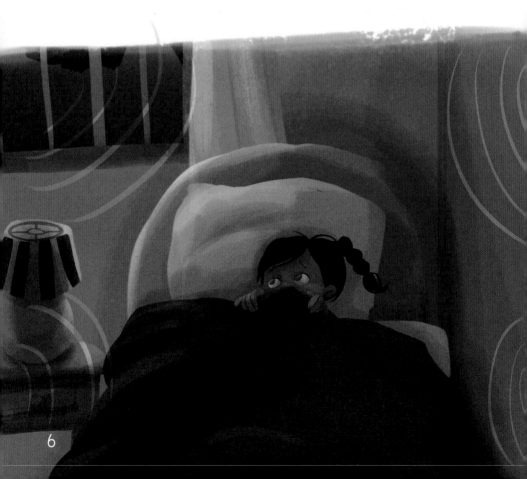

Carmen was trying to sleep in her new yellow room. But her ears would not turn off. She heard something in the new kitchen going *whoosh, whoosh*. She heard something on the new porch going *screak, screak*.

Carlos leaned into Carmen's room. "Are you awake?" he whispered.

"Yes," Carmen said quietly.

"I can't sleep," whispered Carlos.

"Yo tampoco," Carmen whispered back.

"It's really lonely in my room," said Carlos.

"It's really lonely in my room, too," said Carmen.

"Are you thinking what I'm thinking?" they asked at the same time. And, because they were twins, they were.

Chapter 2
Two Sleeping Bags

Carlos and Carmen spread their sleeping bags on the soft carpet in Carmen's new yellow room.

They tried to sleep. But their eyes would not stay shut. And, their ears would not turn off.

"Are you still awake?" whispered Carlos.

"It's not so lonely now, but I still can't sleep," Carmen said.

"Yo tampoco," Carlos agreed.

Then Carlos started to laugh quietly. Carmen began to laugh too.

Carlos looked over at his sister and said, "It's not as quiet now either."

Carlos grinned at Carmen. Carmen smiled back at Carlos. Then they both giggled into their pillows.

"It's hard to go to sleep in a new room," said Carmen.

"It's hard to go to sleep in a new house," said Carlos.

Carlos rolled onto his side. Carmen flopped onto her back.

"I still can't sleep," said Carmen.

"Yo tampoco," said Carlos. Then he added, "I know! I need Poochy-Perro, and you need Gatito."

So, Carlos tiptoed back to his room and got his fluffy brown dog. And, Carmen grabbed her fluffy gray cat off her bed.

"Now we can go to sleep," said Carmen. "We have our fluffies."

"And, we have our sleeping bags," added Carlos.

Then they smiled and said, "And, we have each other."

Chapter 3
Night Noises

Carlos and Carmen were almost
asleep in their sleeping bags.

Suddenly, Carmen sat up and said,
"Did you hear that noise?"

"What noise?" asked Carlos.

Carmen heard the noise again. It was a lonely noise. It was a scary noise. It was a keep-you-from-going-to-sleep noise.

"I just heard the ruido again," whispered Carmen.

"I heard it this time, too," whispered Carlos.

"¿Qué es?" Carmen whispered back.

"Do you think it's a ghost?" asked Carlos.

Carlos grabbed Carmen's hand and squeezed it tightly. Carmen squeezed back just as hard. They scooted close to each other and listened in the dark.

The noise came again. This time it was a sad, spooky noise. Luckily, it was also a not-so-very-close-by noise.

"¿Qué es?" asked Carmen again.

"I don't know," answered Carlos, "but it's giving me the creeps. I think I'll tell Mamá and Papá," he added, giving Carmen's hand an extra squeeze.

"Okay," said Carmen, "but I'll come with you. I don't want to be by myself with that nighttime noise."

Holding hands, Carlos and Carmen walked away from their new rooms and the sad, spooky nighttime noise.

Chapter 4
Spooky

Carlos and Carmen found Mamá and Papá unpacking boxes in the kitchen.

"Mis amores, what is wrong?"
Mamá asked with surprise.

"We can't sleep," said Carmen.

"We keep hearing something sad
and spooky," added Carlos.

"I will go find out what is making
the noise," said Papá.

"Be careful, Papá!" said Carlos. "It might be a ghost."

"Or maybe a monster," added Carmen. "But just a little one."

Papá went outside. Carlos could hear him walking on the deck. Carmen could hear him rustling in the bushes.

"Come here you spooky little monster," said Papá.

When Papá came back in the house, he was holding a wriggling plaid shirt. He had a big smile on his face.

"I found your sad, spooky noise," laughed Papá as he held up his shirt. "It is not a ghost, and it is not a monster. Not even a chiquito one."

Just at that moment, the bundle in the shirt said, *murr-uhhh.*

Carlos looked at Carmen. Carmen looked at Carlos. Then they both looked at Papá, who pulled back the edge of the shirt.

A small black head with pointy ears poked up.

"It's a kitten!" the twins said at the same time. "Can we keep it? Can we? Can we?"

"It can sleep in my room," said Carlos. "And, we can call it Spooky."

"No, Spooky can sleep in my room," said Carmen.

"¡Ya basta!" said Mamá with a laugh. "That's enough. We can keep the gatito tonight, and mañana we will see if it is lost."

"If Spooky doesn't have a home, can we keep her?" asked Carlos.

Mamá and Papá looked at each other.

Spooky asked, *murr-uhhh*?

Papá laughed. "I think her meower is broken, but it's okay with me."

"It's okay with me, too," said Mamá.

"Hooray!" shouted the twins.

Then Carlos and Carmen took the kitten upstairs. The twins wriggled into their sleeping bags. Spooky curled up in the space between them.

Spanish to English

chiquito – very small

gatito – kitten

Mamá – Mommy

mañana – tomorrow

mis amores – my loves

Papá – Daddy

perro – dog

¿Qué es? – What is it?

ruido – noise

¡Ya basta! – That's enough!

yo tampoco – me either